The Three

A. Carys

A. Carys

The characters and events portrayed in this book are fictitious. Any similarity to real persons, living or dead, is coincidental and not intended by the author.

No part of this book may be reproduced, or stored in a retrieval system, or transmitted in any form or by any means, electronic, mechanical, photocopying, recording, or otherwise, without express written permission of the publisher.

Copyright © 2024 A. Carys

All rights reserved.

BOOKS IN THIS SERIES

Of Doors and Betrayal

The Pickpocket and the Princess

The Master, My Wings, Our Service

'Cos This Is How Villains Are Made

A Circus of Wonder

A Sentence to Death

A Deal With The Devil

Let Her Go

The Three

Queen Rory, The Banished

A. Carys

DEDICATION

Initially, this idea came to me just over four years ago, so here's a sneak peek into the story that started it all.

A. Carys

CHAPTER ONE

Sorting through files on the latest movements of the rebels is half boring, half interesting.

As the second eldest son of two of the Leaders of our country, sitting in on official meetings is a requirement. Being in these meetings and in training to become a part of The Six means I have to look through all the reports that have come in overnight. I have to read through all of the information and cherry pick the most important bits and place a highlighted copy in every Results Package. That's why, at the moment, there are loads of stray pieces of paper scattered on the table in front of me. After another hour of work, I put together the final Results Package before grabbing the stapler next to me, but in the process of taking hold of it I knock a small stack of files onto the floor, files that had been precariously balanced on the edge of the table.

"Shit." I slide off my chair and onto my knees to pick them up. I pick them up one by one, collecting them in my hand before placing them back on the table.

"You know, you can stay seated in your chair when I enter a room. No need to get on your knees," says Ivy as she walks into the meeting room.

I roll my eyes as I sit down in my chair, placing the hastily collected files back on the table.

"Lovely to see you." I reach for her, but she dodges my hands and takes a seat in the chair next to me.

She smiles as I take hold of the metal edges of her chair and pull her to me, her legs then squished between mine. We both lean forward, our hands coming together, and I gently press a kiss to her forehead. She follows that with a quick peck of my lips before sitting back in her chair.

"Missed you," she says.

"I missed you too. Didn't think you were getting back for another few days."

She shrugs. "The analysts didn't have as much data as they thought. It was strange since they should have buckets of data considering everything that's been happening, but they said to go back in a week, and they should have all the data we need."

I nod and quickly scribble down what she just said as it's something that looks to be worth mentioning during the meeting.

"Did you think about the offer?" I ask her as I put down my pen and start sorting out the files that fell on the floor.

"I didn't. Being a Leader isn't something I want, I want to work with the data," she says, wringing her hands. I grab her hands, holding onto them to stop her from hurting herself.

"That's fine, Iv, you don't need to do anything that makes you uncomfortable. But you need to think about who will take over your spot, your brother isn't old enough to be considered at the moment."

She nods. "I know. But that's something I've also been thinking about. What if I took on the role of being one of The Three, but I worked on handling data?"

"What do you mean?"

"You and Drew are quite capable of leading the country, and I'd still be a Leader with you, but I wouldn't be in the public eye as much as you two would. I would attend the Leader meetings, but I could be the go to for all of the facts. A liaison between the Leaders and the analysts, it would work better than having someone sort through all of the papers before each meeting and another working alongside the analysts."

I take a second to think about what she said. Ivy has always been more than happy to sit in a lab. She's happier when she's running tests or sorting out the data from the Citizen Surveys that come in every month. She's clever, resourceful, and would be an asset if she took on the responsibilities from her parents.

"I know you don't want to be in the media or heading up campaigns like our parents, but we would be different. Once we're in charge, we can run the country however we see fit. A lot of the stuff at the moment is for transparency so that the citizens know that we're taking the threats from the rebels seriously.

I know you'll say that you just don't want to do it but think about it. Please?"

She rolls her eyes, knowing for a fact that she won't change her answer. "Fine. Anyway, that's not why I came here today."

I perk up, turning fully away from the table.

"What did you bring?" I ask as she picks her bag up from the floor and places it on her lap. She pulls out one book, and then another, placing both of them on the table.

"More reality waste," she says, placing her bag back on the floor.

"Reality waste?"

"The few things that fall through the cracks of one reality and into another. Theorists have claimed this can happen, and we've been seeing more of it fall through recently. These two books were found yesterday evening." She pulls one book toward her and flicks through the pages.

"You're not going to catch anything from them, right? I don't need to worry about trying to cure an incurable disease?"

She laughs. "No, you don't need to worry at all.

Lab techs thoroughly examined them for harmful and contagious bacteria, and they came back clear."

I nod. "Does it say where they came from?" I ask as I pick up the second book and examine it.

"According to the techs, the one I'm holding is meant to be part of an archive from a place called Tevia Viselle. It's written on the front page." She opens the book to the front page and points out the scribbling letters that tell us where it came from. "And there's clear signs of whoever owned it adding in pages at the beginning. You can see here from the way binding isn't as clean cut as it would normally be that these first two or three pages were added in at a later date."

I'm aware I'm no longer looking at the book in Ivy's hands. Instead, I'm staring at her as I listen to her ramble about these books and the other realities. She takes me through how they actually fall through and that every reality, apparently, has some kind of neutral ground that all the artefacts land on. And that's where these books were found and some other bits that Ivy has yet to examine.

She's smart when it comes to these kinds of

things. Her brain is like a sponge because, somehow, she manages to absorb so much information in such a short amount of time.

The door to the meeting room opens and we both startle, quickly moving to cover up the books.

"Good morning Ivy, morning Lor," says my mother as she walks to her designated seat.

"Morning, Mrs Bridger," Ivy says as she carefully puts the books away in her bag.

"Will you be staying for the meeting?"

"Of course. I've brought this week's analyst reports and I thought I could take you all through them," Ivy says.

"That sounds like a wonderful idea. Everyone else will be here soon."

We both nod as we wait for my father and the other Leaders to arrive.

CHAPTER TWO

When the rest of the Leaders arrive, I hand out the Results Packages.

They all flick through the papers, using their highlighters and pens to take further notes and pinpoint their talking points.

The next thing I do is fill each cup with water, from the pitcher I'd brought with me earlier, before retaking my seat. I tuck my chair into the gap under the table before looking at the Results Package I'd left for myself.

"To start with, I'd like to focus on the Citizen Surveys," Mac, my father, announces as he flicks to the front of his package.

"I agree. Citizen Survey feedback has taken a backseat lately due to the rebellious activity of The

Three," Molly says, and everyone nods in agreement.

The Three. A group of three rebels who have made themselves known to us, but also somehow completely invisible. The motivations behind their opposition to the current leaders is unknown, but they're dangerous, nonetheless. *Isaac Vincent. Marshall Ackroyd. Leanna Fitch Tucker*. Three completely unproblematic citizens until three years ago, and none of us can figure out why.

"Lornan, why don't you take us through the Citizen files. It'll be good practice," Ethan, Ivy's father, offers. I nod and pull my Results Package toward me. I flip to the Citizens section before putting my glasses on.

"When I was putting together these Packages, I noted some changes in the Citizen Statements at the end of Survey. This particular Statement raised a few alarm bells for me since this person's statements have been consistent over the last year. We don't have the name of the person, but we have their Survey ID and they've made it clear that the rebel activity has reached their area."

"What area of the country?" asks my mother.

"Krover. An Outer City in the west where we've been seeing an increase in activity. The patrols we've placed out there seem to be noting this as well and have requested a formal meeting with yourselves."

Everyone nods.

"Very good. Have them come into the Capital on Thursday and we'll have a chat with them," my father says, and I quickly jot it down in my post-meeting notebook. "Now, why don't you take us through the electric company reports."

I nod and grab the letter from the electrical company. "They said that they had a look at the area in which the outages were happening, but they couldn't see anything out of place. Despite that though, they said they were going to continue to monitor the electric usage and get back to us with any findings."

Next to me, Ivy raises her hand.

"If I may interrupt. I've been with the analysts the last couple of days, and they have a strong feeling the patterns of when the outages happen correlate with when The Three are present in the area. Techere has had a lot of outages in the last few weeks and from the information we've collected it would seem likely that they have their base of operations there."

"How can they have their base there? We've patrols regularly checking the Identification Papers and House Registries. Surely we'd know by now if they were there?" Amelia, Ethan's wife, asks.

"That's the thing, they aren't actually staying in Techere, they're staying around it. They're harvesting the electricity from Techere and into their own living arrangement. From the charts that record the flow of the electricity being provided by each town, they show that The Three may be hiding out in the Rysyll Mountain range." Ivy gets up and hands out printed copies of the charts.

Everyone nods as they look at the charts.

"What would you recommend, Ivy, to prevent this from happening?" I ask.

She turns to look at me, looking pleased with herself. "I would recommend that we don't do anything drastic that would lead The Three to figuring out that we know where they are. They thrive off of keeping us on our toes. My recommendation would be to leave them alone for the time being, but we should continue to closely monitor Techere and the Rysyll Mountains so that we can build a picture of their daily routine."

"Good. I like that suggestion, thank you, Ivy," my father says as his watch beeps. He looks down at it just as the rest of the Leader's watches go off. "Ah, it seems we are needed elsewhere. If you two can collate the important information into a couple of pages and post them in our pigeonholes by this evening, that would be a great help," my father asks as he collects his blazer and Leader Pack.

"Of course," I say with a nod.

I start collecting all of the packs we haven't been through yet and place them in the mesh file holders for safe keeping. I tidy the table of the remaining papers and place them in a different mesh tray before tidying away the cups of water.

While Ivy waits for me, she tucks in the chairs and closes the blinds. As we leave the room, I turn the lights off and then lock the door once it's shut. We head toward the common room where we start sorting out the important information from the meeting.

CHAPTER THREE

Ivy and I spent the majority of yesterday afternoon collating the information from the meeting into a package of three, succinctly written pages. It took far longer than it should have, but we were done by the final staff dinner call, so we managed to get something to eat before we headed to bed.

"Lor, you look shattered," Wren, my little sister, comments as she shuts her locker.

"I feel it. Do you know how long it takes to create succinct information pages for thirty Citizen Surveys and ten pages of Results Packages?"

"Didn't you have Ivy with you?" she asks.

"I did, but it still takes a long time. We didn't post the packages until eleven."

"Well, the next meeting isn't for a month, so we

have some time to sleep before then," Ivy chimes in from beside me.

"Good god," I say, startled from not noticing her arrival.

"Definitely not god, but I can be if you want me to," she says, clearly flirting with me in obvious revenge for the *incident* last week. A slightly romantic incident that we do not speak of because it is *far too embarrassing* for Ivy to even think about; her words, not mine. And I know that she used her visit to the Analysts to avoid me and the conversation I wanted to have with her, one that I don't think we'll ever have because she can always sense it coming.

I laugh and wrap an arm around her shoulder, pulling her into me. I place a kiss on the top of her head and tell her that I won't be calling her god, ever.

"How about some lunch?" Kian suggests and everyone nods.

We head to the cafeteria, joining the queue of students. We talk about the classes from the day and Wren complains that both Ivy and I get a day off on Mondays, which isn't technically true because we work with our parents. As the children of the

Buchanan and Bridger Leaders, we are required to work alongside them one day a week. Drew Whitely, eldest child and only son of Molly and Fin Whitely, sometimes works with us on our Mondays in the office, but he normally works on Thursdays since that's the day his parents choose to work in the offices instead of in their apartment.

"Do you want to go to the roof?" Ivy asks as I pick up my tray.

I raise an eyebrow. "What do you have?"

"Something great."

I smile and lean over to Wren and tell her that Ivy and I are needed elsewhere. It isn't uncommon for us to be called upon during school hours by the Admins of the school or our parents, but it also isn't something that happens frequently. So when Ivy and I want to sneak off, that's what we tell everyone.

We leave the cafeteria, bidding goodbye to our group. We head for the back building of the school. We climb up the old stairs and move toward our favourite darkened corner where no one will be able to see us.

"What have you got?"

"An exclusive look at the Identification videos of The Three," she says with great excitement as she opens her sandwich.

"The what?" I question as she pulls out her tablet.

"Identification videos. We've only ever had their names and the first names of their children. But now we have their faces, full names and picture identity of their children too. Take a look."

She hands me the tablet and I watch the grainy footage of three people working on the electrical boxes on the outskirts of Techere.

"That's how they are diverting the power? Tampering with the electrical boxes?"

"Sort of. They're taking those cables, the ones in their hands and working them through the outer sands, trailing them between their hideout and the electrical boxes. I've watched this video so many times to see if I can see any footage of their base, but unfortunately the cameras don't quite reach the Mountains."

I laugh and hand her back the tablet. "You'd make a great Leader, yesterday in the meeting and your dedication to these videos proves it."

She sighs and shakes her head. "Let–"

She's cut off by the bell, signalling the end of lunch. I smile and stand up, offering her my hand. She takes it, using it to pull herself up. Ivy then grabs her bag from the floor and smooths down her skirt before following me toward the stairs.

CHAPTER FOUR

The afternoon passes by relatively slowly.

Ivy and I narrowly made the start of our first class after lunch. Although we didn't spend much time focusing on the classwork since we decided to work on figuring out how we could strategically place more Military members and patrols within the Techere area. Ivy uses her mother's log in to gain access to the patrols that have already been placed in Techere, but no matter how many times we rearrange the patrols or switch them with normal citizens, we know that The Three will know that something has changed.

"Their profiles are detailed. They went through the psychological training trials back when the Academy was thinking about adding it to the final year's specialist options. They have extensive knowledge and field training. They're top of their game in every possible area of what we would class as *war tactics*."

"So we can't get near them in any way because they'll, what, automatically know?"

"Pretty much. I have a small group of analysts running simulations on the best way to get close to them."

"Are they having any luck?"

She shakes her head. "They've run half a dozen simulations already, a lot of them are similar to what we've been trying. We won't be able to do anything without gaining their attention. The only thing we could consider trying is recruiting someone who already lives in Techere, specifically someone who lives near the mountains; but it's likely The Three know a lot about the people living in close quarters to them so we'd have to be extremely careful."

"It's something we could pitch to our parents. It's not a crazy idea."

She nods, and the ringing of the bell signals the end of class. We grab our bags and head out of the classroom, following the crowd into the hallways. Ivy is still tapping at her tablet as we reach our lockers. She leans against hers while I open mine and pull out three books that I'll need for class later.

"Well, well, well, Lornan Buchanan and Ivy Bridger. What a pleasant surprise," says Silas as he and his group of friends, including my eldest brother Eli, crowd around us.

I don't know what our family ever did to Eli, but he seems to have something against the fact that he is a Leader's son. He spends hours outside of the compound, hanging around with Silas and his group of *interesting* friends. He doesn't talk to me anymore, if I see him in the halls of the compound, I'll say hello and in return he just grunts. It hurts every time, we were so close as kids, but since he started mixing with Silas last year, we've grown apart. We're practically strangers now and I hate it.

"How is it that you two can sit there and whisper throughout our classes and not get told off? And how come you get to carry tablets around with you and the rest of us can't?" he asks, stepping closer to us. Out of the corner of my eye, I see Ivy cower and cradle her tablet to her chest. I make a move to stand in front of her, keeping her out of Silas's reach.

"Aww, poor Ivy. She needs her protector to keep her safe," he taunts as he tries to step around me and grab at Ivy. He's always been fixated on her for some reason, whenever he sees her he feels the need to try and grab her wrist or sling his arm around her shoulders. He thinks it's funny, but for Ivy it's torture. It took me close to a year to gain Ivy's trust enough for me to be able to touch her, to even just touch her hand. She only permits myself and her parents to touch her. She told me that having people touch her makes her skin crawl. I guess Silas knows this since he always tries to make contact, and I'd fathom a guess that Eli is the one who told him.

I grab his wrist in retaliation and push him away.

"Leave her alone, Silas."

His group *oohs* and *aahs* as he steps closer to me again. I stand up straighter in recognition of the challenge, refusing to back down.

"And what are you going to do if I don't?"

"I'll–"

"Why don't we break this up. There's no need to start a fight, especially when the Admins are watching," says Kian as he gets in the middle of Silas and I.

Silas pauses for a moment, but steps away from Kian.

"Watch yourself Buchanan, who knows how soon we'll be seeing each other."

I turn and stare at him, trying not to let the confusion of his words show on my face.

None of us move until he and his group have disappeared around the corner. Once I'm sure they're on their way to their class, I pull Ivy round to my front and hold her close.

"You okay?" I ask.

She nods but doesn't look up at me. I take a deep breath and link my fingers through hers. She might not be speaking right now but I know what she needs. Despite her bubbly personality, Ivy is deeply shy and closed off. But my main concern right now is that she doesn't normally shut down like this when Silas tries his usual tricks, but she seems to be struggling to maintain what she calls her *grip*. She hates losing it and right now, class doesn't seem like the best place to take her.

I look at Kian and he nods, knowing exactly what I'm thinking.

"See you at home," I say as I pull Ivy toward the back of the school, fully intending to spend the rest of the afternoon on the roof.

CHAPTER FIVE

Silas's threat has sat in the pit of my stomach for the last week and a half. It's been drawing my anxiety to it, feeding itself on my worry and getting bigger. I've reported his threat to my parents, especially since Ivy discovered the connection between Silas and one of The Three.

Apparently his uncle is Isaac Vincent. After confirming their identities, we were able to look into all of their relatives, friends and associates. We've managed to build a better picture of their network and we've been working on identifying who they would be most likely to contact. We have a few leads so far which we're going to be following up on in the next few weeks. Ivy has spent the last few days trawling the Identification servers to see if she can find out how deep the connection between Silas and Isaac goes. She's not found a great deal of information so far, but she's digging up quite a bit of information on the Vincent family that'll be useful to us in the future.

"Hey, Dad wants us," Kian says as he pops his head around my bedroom door.

"Where?" I respond as I put down my tablet and shuffle across my bed.

"Our main common," he says before disappearing.

Okay, I think to myself as I grab my jacket from the back of my desk chair. The place that we live can't be classed as a house. It's too big to be called that. We refer to it as a compound since there's a lot of areas inside of it. The building is made of three large, square buildings, all of which are connected by corridors and hidden hallways. Each building has two floors, the top floor is for living and the bottom floor is for working. Since there are six Leaders (there were originally three Leaders, but when they got married, their spouse became a Leader too) it made sense for each family to get one building.

I head over to my closet. I open the doors and

push my clothes to the side. I press the back wall of the closet and it opens, revealing a hidden hallway which will take me to the Main Common. Each building has a Main Common Room that sits in the centre of the top floor. Each Main Common is decorated the same, long sofas, two oak wood coffee tables with matching cabinets around the edges of the room. Plush red carpet that your shoes sink into covers the floor, it's quite useful that the carpet is so spongy because it allows for sneaking in late to the meetings.

I push against the first door I come to before quietly slipping onto the sofa next to Ivy. Our hips are pressed right against each other. Ivy looks up at me with a smile.

"You're late," she scolds, whispering.

"Only by a few seconds," I respond as she shakes her head.

I smile at the back of her head as she turns back to face our parents. This girl has me wrapped around her finger, always has and always will. It took her a few hours to recover from the incident with Silas, we spent the rest of the school day on the roof. We sat there, not talking, not investigating anything on the tablet, we just sat. I'd sat against the brickwork of the edge of the roof, the shade keeping us hidden. Ivy sat in between my legs, her back against my chest with her eyes closed. Since the incident, she's returned to her usual bubbly and sassy self.

"Concentrate," she whispers as she jabs me in the ribs with her elbow.

"Yes ma'am."

"–However, that doesn't mean that you can try to trick us into thinking you're going to one place when in fact you are going somewhere else. There will be none of that now that The Three have been spotted in the Capital and in a rented motorhome park in Haldver. Understand?" Drew's father, Fin, announces.

All of us nod.

"What Fin told you is all the information we have on The Three's current location. They seem to be making their way closer to the Capital so we've decided that now it is the time to show you the place you can go if The Three ever make it into this building. It's a place that has been built and stocked with everything you would need to survive should you ever need to go there."

"Where is it?" asks Dalia, Drew's fifteen year old sister.

"We're going to show you. Come come," Ivy's mother says as she gestures for us all to follow her.

Everyone gets up and follows her. All of our parents are up front, quietly discussing things between themselves. Ivy and I head up the back. Instead of talking, Ivy is tapping away at her tablet again while I take a headcount.

Drew, Dalia and Desi at the front with Desi being carried by Dalia.

Ivy is next to me while Calum walks in front of her.

Kian and Wren are walking in the middle of the group. I look around for Eli, but he's nowhere to be seen. I shouldn't be surprised, he's not one for hanging around with his family, but I would've thought my parents might have gotten through to him by now. Haven't they noticed the absence of their eldest son? I worry about him. He's still my brother and I want him to be safe, but I fear that if the time arose for him to pick sides, we wouldn't be the side he chooses.

"Behind this door is a staircase. It will take you down to a place very far underground," my father says as he unlocks the door using a keypad.

"This is something we have been working on for a while now. We've been digging out this safe haven for you all for the last year and half. If you end up going down there, you will need to follow every other right for four rights before taking every left until you reach a vault-like door," says Amelia as she pulls a map out of a wall panel.

"This will be what you need to use if you need to get to the safe haven. Upon scanning your thumb on the biometric print scanner, the door will open for you. Upon closing it, you will need the most senior of you to initiate the automatic deadbolt and door lock nullifying system," my mother says as she shows us the map in closer detail.

"What is the classification for most senior?" Dalia asks.

"The most senior links to the person who is the highest rank of which Ivy, Lornan and Drew are the most senior. Now, only one of you needs to activate the nullifying system. Once you've scanned your thumb, the walls around the door will seal themselves shut permanently. You won't be able to exit through that way again and no one will be able to enter," my mother explains.

"But won't they be able to find us from the surface? Ground penetrating radar would give them our location, no?" Ivy asks with a raise of her hand.

"Actually, it won't. What we have built is completely undetectable. The only way out, if you choose to seal the entrance door, is through a derelict house out in Airies. You will be the future of this country, and in order to ensure that we created this safe haven for you," my father explains.

"The only thing we need you to do is pack go bags and one rucksack worth of valuables you don't want to lose. Please take the rest of this afternoon to do that before bringing them to us. We'll then show you where you can store them for easy accessibility."

We all nod before each of us grabs a duffel bag from our parents. The bags smell and have clearly just been brought. As we head back to our rooms to pack our go-bags, I grab Ivy's wrist, signalling for her to hold back.

"What?" she murmurs.

"They're scared."

"Aren't we all? The Three are unpredictable, they'd be stupid if they weren't scared."

"I'm telling you; something is going to happen, and they know it."

"So?"

"So we need to be ready."

"I am ready."

"Good," I say as we start walking back to our rooms. I don't say to her that I don't feel ready, not in the slightest.

CHAPTER SIX

Things have been quiet.

Too quiet.

Silas has been keeping out of our way at school, and we've not seen much of Eli either. Not at school or at home which has raised some eyebrows around the house. I'm not even sure if he's been coming home at night anymore.

Meanwhile, our parents have been running drills similar to that of a fire drill. They set off the new alarm system they've had installed and make us practise getting up and getting to the door that leads to the tunnels. So far, we've all made a good effort with it. We've all managed to get out in good time which would give us a head start on anyone pursuing us.

"Do you really think that they'll attack us?" Wren

asks. She's sitting on the sofa in the meeting room I'm in.

"They might. We can't really be sure of anything right now so try not to let it worry you."

"But what if they do? Isn't that something you think about?" she reasons as she unfolds herself from the sofa and makes her way over to me.

"I won't lie to you and say I'm not worried, because I am. But if I let that worry consume me, I'll be useless. I don't want you to worry too much either. I know that's easier said than done, but worrying about the ifs won't help you right now."

She takes a deep breath and nods. "I'll try."

"That's all I ask."

She seems to hesitate for a second, her mouth opening and then closing again.

"You okay?" I ask.

"What about Eli?" she blurts.

"What about him?"

"What will he do if we're all hidden away, and he comes looking?"

I sigh. "He isn–"

I'm cut off by the room shaking as a loud boom

sounds from somewhere to the right of us. I jump out of my chair and grab Wren, quickly dragging her under the table. I hold her against me until the rumbling stops, my hand covering the top of her head protectively. There's not a lot of extra furniture in this meeting room, but the few decorative picture frames fall from the walls and the glasses and pitches of water rumble, falling over from the force of the shaking.

"What's going on?" she asks.

"I've no idea, but we need to go make sure everyone is alright," I say as I crawl out from under the table now that the shaking has stopped.

I offer my hand to her; she takes it, and we rush head out of the meeting and right toward the unmistakable smell of burning.

"Thank god you guys are alright," my father says as he pulls both my mother and Amelia behind him.

"Are you all okay?" I ask as I try to do a visual assessment for injuries.

"We're all fine, Desi, Ethan, Molly, Fin and Kian are all fine as well. Drew is still at school with Dalia, but Ivy is still in there," he says, and my brain instantly locks on the thoughts of Ivy being trapped.

"Where?" I demand as I shed my jacket and roll up the sleeves of my top.

"No, son, it's too dangerous. You'll get hurt," my dad says but I ignore him.

I make a beeline for the now ruined doorway, pushing through the rubble on the floor and covering my nose and mouth with my top.

"Ivy?" I yell out into the wreck.

The Main Common is in bits. Parts of the walls have caved in and there are small fires burning away at the curtains and furniture. I make quick work of stamping them out with my shoe. I check under fallen bits of rubble before making my way to the shared dining room.

"Ivy?" I call out as I try to wave away the dust from in front of my eyes.

"Lornan?" A small voice calls out to me, and I spin to the right.

Ivy is leaning against one of the walls. She's covered in soot and dust and her arm is trapped under a smouldering piece of support beam. I rush to her and make quick work of moving the beam, showing little care for the way my skin tingles from the heat. I chuck it to the side and quickly check Ivy's arm.

She cries out when I move it. Definitely broken, not all of it but definitely some of it, and the skin around it doesn't look too good either. It's raw, bright red and angry looking as the wound continues to grow. I move my hand down her arm and check her hand which is one hundred percent broken, that I can tell for sure.

"I'm sorry sweetheart, I know it hurts," I say as I move some of the extra pieces of rubble that are surrounding her.

She cries out and tries to pull back and curl up into the wall. I don't let her as I grab her good arm and get ready to help her.

"Come on, be careful now," I say as I help her up and guide her out of the room. As we move away from the destroyed room, firefighters run in and start putting out the small fires that are still burning.

I bring Ivy out into the corridor, and we are instantly met by paramedics. They take Ivy from me, trying to guide her down the stairs and into the makeshift medical area, but she refuses to let go of my hand, so I have no choice but to go with them.

I stay by her side as they examine her arm. She cries and whimpers as they treat and wrap the burns. They then work on a cast for her hand after doing a portable x-ray. They confirm that the skin from her elbow to her wrist is burnt, and, unfortunately, her hand is broken. They test her movements, and she can slightly move her fingers which I take as a good sign. They tell her not to use her left arm too much and to try and keep the pressure off her fingers and wrist.

"She'll be okay?" I ask as the paramedics pack up their kits.

"Yes. If you can help her keep her burns clean, treated and wrapped, they should heal well. Unfortunately, we cannot guarantee that there won't be any scarring, but we believe she'll regain most movement in her fingers and elbow."

"But not her wrist?"

"The burns around her wrist are the worst and like I said, we can't guarantee that there won't be any scarring."

I nod. "Thank you."

The paramedic smiles before taking her bag and

walking away.

As soon as all of the emergency services clear out, everyone starts checking on one another. Our parents do a headcount alongside double checking that Drew and Dalia were at the school, which they were.

Everyone else escaped relatively unscathed, it seems that Ivy came out with the worst of the injuries. And as everyone heads to bed after having the army come in and secure the destroyed rooms, I decide to spend the night with Ivy in her room.

After I change into my pyjamas and do my business in the bathroom, I help Ivy get ready for bed. I help her get her smoke ruined jumper off and replace it with her night shirt, or should I say one of my old, way too large for her t-shirts that she stole from me. I help her unbuckle the belt of her trousers and let her shimmy out of them as I grab her new underwear. I lay them on the end of her bed and turn my back to give her some privacy. After she's changed, we head to the bathroom, and I help her wash her face before squeezing some toothpaste on her toothbrush.

While she finishes up in the bathroom, I sort her

bed. I move one of her cushions and place it down on her preferred side of the double bed before pulling back the covers. Ivy comes out of the bathroom and settles straight into bed, laying down on her back and placing her left arm on the cushion. I climb in beside her and take hold of her right hand.

"Try to get some sleep," I tell her.

"You won't leave, will you?"

I shake my head. "No. I'll be right here when you wake up."

Seemingly satisfied with that answer, she closes her eyes. I wait until her breathing is steady before trying to fall asleep myself.

CHAPTER SEVEN

In the days that follow the attack, we all work hard on plans to keep the citizens of New Esalca safe.

I've been staying with Ivy every night, and I've been glued to her side during the day as per her request. I know she's worried something like that will happen again, and with Silas doubling down on his terrorising, she's shutting down a lot more and I'm worried about her. Thankfully though, as soon as we get home, we escape to her room and take some time to decompress.

Other than that, life has been hectic. While we've been allowed to return to school, we've been given revised timetables which see us in school from eleven till two, with another three hours private tutoring at the compound.

"Are you ready for the broadcast?" my mother asks as she fiddles with the collar of my shirt. The Leaders have decided to do a broadcast to the whole of New Esalca to update them on the situation with The Three. They decided this was the best move after more than 10 individual journalists requested statements.

"Yes," I say as I bat at her hands. "Stop fussing, I'm more than capable of dressing myself."

"I know you are honey, but things have been hectic lately and fussing over my children is a good distraction," she admits.

I nod and pull her in for a hug. She sighs and I feel her head rest against my shoulder. She needed this, because when she pulls away at the sound of my father entering the room her eyes shine brighter than they were a few moments ago. I know she worries about all of us, she's been the best mother anyone could ever ask for, but the attack on the compound spooked her, more so than the rest of the Leaders. She gives me a grateful smile before rushing over to my father. I watch them for a moment before my attention is drawn to Ivy as she walks into the room. I go over to her and wrap an arm around her shoulder, pressing her good side against me.

"How are you feeling?" I ask as we move over and stand behind our parents who are seated in front of the camera.

"Okay. A lot better than yesterday."

"I'm happy to hear it," I say and press a gentle kiss to the top of her head. I'm about to say something else when my father shushes everyone as they get ready to begin the broadcast.

My mother is the one to start the broadcast. She thanks the citizens for tuning in before she begins explaining what happened and the reason for the broadcast before letting Molly take over.

"We, as your Leaders, are bound to do what is right for all of you. And we wouldn't be doing our jobs properly if we didn't work to protect you all. While I understand if you think these measures are extreme, we have decided to implement the following protective measures for not only our piece of mind, but yours as well," Amelia explains before letting her husband start speaking.

"As of tomorrow evening, an eight-o-clock curfew will come into force for all citizens. Anyone found outside of their homes after this time will be questioned and could face being arrested by patrols in the area. We have also implemented a new rule that will require all citizens to carry their Identification papers on them at all times, especially when moving between towns."

"If there are any complaints or queries, please direct them toward our inquiry line. There will be more information coming out over the next few days with ways you can ensure you are following the new rules and regulations," my father says, closing off the broadcast.

Once the broadcast manager confirms that they've stopped broadcasting, we all move away, spreading out around the room. My father gives out a set of orders to a Patrol Leader based on the information given out in the broadcast. The Patrol Leader salutes my father before leaving, my father then turns to Ivy, Drew and I.

He gives us the assignment of programming the new identification panels that will feature on each town border, while Wren, Dalia and Kian are told to distribute the new electra-blades to the military groups who will be patrolling the town borders.

Programming the identification panels takes most of the day. It keeps the three of us preoccupied and keeps us swapping from the meeting room we're doing the programming in and the testing lab. We work until late evening and despite the deep, sleepy ache I feel in my bones, I keep working well into the early hours of the morning. We need to figure out how to keep the citizens safe while simultaneously figuring out how to stop The Three, so sleep is low down on my list of priorities.

CHAPTER EIGHT

The Three have been quiet and unseen for the last three weeks. They initially went to ground after the attack on the compound, but they were spotted again heading out to the Rysyll Mountain Range and haven't been seen since.

"We'll meet again tomorrow to continue this discussion," my father says as he closes up his folder. At the moment, our hands are tied. There's not a lot we can do, so having these official meetings is becoming pointless.

Everyone nods and says variations of *see you tomorrow* before leaving the room. I stay behind and wait for Ivy to finish packing up her stuff. She's struggling to stuff her papers in her bag, but I stay silent. The first time I offered to help her tidy up her papers, she nearly bit my head off. Understandably so because since the accident-but-not-actually-an-accident, people have been doting on her all the time, taking away jobs from her because they think she can't do it one handed and that pisses her off. While she doesn't mind clinging to me, having me help her with making food or getting ready for bed, she hates people taking tasks away from her at work. And if people saw me stepping in and not being asked to leave her alone, then they might think that they need to step in as well.

"Stop staring at me," she says without looking at me.

"Sorry," I mutter and move to collect up the leftover folders. I sort them into the filing cabinet and by the time I turn around, Ivy is ready and waiting for me.

I take her good hand and we walk out of meeting room two. We don't follow the sound of clattering plates and busy chatter of dinner happening down the hallway in the Bridger Building, instead, we head for the roof. We climb the fire exit stairs and settle on the old, probably internally mouldy, swinging chair.

I take a deep breath of the fresh night air before closing my eyes and leaning my head back. My whole body feels heavy, and I think I could fall asleep here if I tried hard enough.

"Are you okay?" Ivy asks.

I nod as I open my eyes and stare at the sky. "Tired."

"Do you think you're taking on too much?"

I shake my head. "I don't think I'm sleeping as well as I could be, but I'll be okay."

She nods, but I know she isn't convinced by my answer. "You're not sleeping well because you're watching me, aren't you?"

"What makes you think that?"

"Lor, I wake up in the night and you might've dozed off, but you'll be looking down at me with your head propped up."

I sigh. "I worry about you Ivy. The attack a few weeks ago could have been so much worse. And if it had been any worse, then I could've lost you," I admit.

She sighs and I feel her shuffle closer, moving my arm out of the way and around her shoulders. She snuggles up to me before looking me in the eyes.

"You wouldn't have lost me, and the attack was only as bad as The Three wanted it to be. I don't think the aim was to kill anyone, only injure so that we would panic and try to control everything around us."

I raise an eyebrow. "Are you quoting your predictive analysis work to me right now?"

"Of course, giving you facts and statistics seems to be the only way to keep you calm and level."

"Swear to me you won't get in the way of danger if all of this comes to ahead. I can't have you getting hurt or worse, killed."

"I swear," she says as she takes my hand and squeezes it. "I swear to you I'll stay out of danger where possible."

"Good," I say and press a kiss to the top of her head.

We sit there in silence for a while, just enjoying the cool air and the starry sky. Ivy's head rests against my shoulder and she dozes off. I must doze off as well, because the next time my eyes are open, I'm jumping up from the swinging chair, my attention drawn by the blaring alarm coming from inside of the

The Three

building.

CHAPTER NINE

Ivy and I rush across the roof and into the stairwell. We rush down the stairs and into the chaos of everyone on the move.

"What's going on?" I ask as I start running alongside Dalia.

"The Three are here. They've breached the– the ground floor with what we think is– is a small army," she pants as we run toward the bedrooms.

"Seriously?" Ivy asks as we burst into the bedroom area.

"Yes. We need to go now, before they breach any of the other levels," she says as she heads for Desi's room.

Ivy and I head for our own siblings' bedrooms. Wren is already grabbing her coat and personal rucksack when I burst into her room. Once Wren rushes past me, I run to Kian's room. He is, somehow, still asleep until I yank the duvet off him and wake him up. He grumbles but moves quickly to get his personal rucksack. I leave him to make his own way to the tunnels as I pop back into my own room and grab my jacket and the personal rucksack left by my door. I run back out in the main area and all of us stand together.

"Where are the go-bags?" Dalia asks.

"They're down in the safe haven," Drew says, and we all start moving.

"Lor. Lornan help," Ivy calls from behind me.

"Everyone head down to the safe haven, we won't be far behind," I tell them, and they all run off.

I turn and find that she is trying to carry Calum. I dive over to her and take Calum from her arms. He's heavily sleeping and instantly cuddles up and gets comfortable. I make sure she has her rucksack before grabbing her good hand and pulling her behind me. We quickly catch up with the others and head in the direction of the main common in the hopes of finding our parents.

Our parents are there, all of them looking out of the windows and down at the grounds around us. And Eli stands behind them, just staring as well.

"What's going on?" I ask, breaking the silence.

My father is the first one to turn around.

"The Three are here, and we are severely outnumbered. Eli has offered us the best course of action," he says, coming toward us.

"What kind of course of action has he offered you?" Ivy asks.

"The kind that ensures we all make it out alive."

I shake my head. "He's friends with the enemy's nephew, he can't be trusted," I yell as a boom from below shakes the building. I place Calum, who's now awake, on his feet and he runs to Ivy.

"We don't have time to argue about this, Lornan. You need to take everyone to the safe haven now before it's too late. If you can't place your trust in him, then place your trust in us," my mother says as she comes over and hugs me.

"But he is friends with Silas. He's on their side."

"He isn't, not really at least. We don't have time to get into all of the details, but Eli is on our side. But right now, you need to get everyone underground. Let us take it from here and one day, we will all be reunited. I promise you," my mother explains to us all.

I want to argue with her. I want to tell her that she's wrong and that Eli is going to get us killed because I don't trust him, but the look in my mother's eyes says otherwise. My mother has never steered us wrong, so I do as she says.

"Come on, let's go. Head straight toward the safe haven entrance," I say as I start to usher everyone toward the door.

"Lornan," says Eli as he grabs my wrist. "I have no interest in being friends with Silas, but–"

"I don't want to hear it," I say, trying to pull my wrist from his grip.

"Please," he begs.

I don't say anything as the building rumbles, and he takes that opportunity to start talking.

"When information came through that Silas was in frequent contact with his uncle, myself and The Six decided that I needed to try and infiltrate Silas's group."

"You could've told me."

"I couldn't have told you. You'd have made it obvious that we were still on good terms, and the lies I had to feed Silas would've fallen apart the second you looked at him with disgust and at me with knowing."

I swallow thickly. "I doubted you."

He nods, his features turning sympathetic. "I know, but it was what I wanted, what I needed. If you hated me then I knew the others would too. They all look up to you, and one day you'll make the perfect Leader."

I nod, suddenly feeling emotional and I don't know why. "Good luck, Eli."

He nods, a smile pulling at the corners of his mouth.

"Good luck little brother."

CHAPTER TEN

When I walk away from my parents and Eli, I rush to join the others at the entrance to the safe haven.

Just as I enter the tunnels, another boom sounds, it shakes the ground beneath our feet and bits of dust crumble from the doorway to the tunnel. Everyone cowers and covers their heads until the rumbling stops.

"Right, everyone go to the main door," I say as I usher them further into the tunnel. "Drew and I will catch you up."

Ivy and Kian work on ushering the younger siblings over to the main door of the safe haven. Drew and I quickly shut the first door, pulling it closed and twisting the wheel lock mechanism. We twist until the door makes a *clunk* sound, which indicates that it's locked, before re-joining the others at the actual entrance to the safe haven.

Wren puts in the code to open the door and it clicks open with a hiss. She ushers everyone inside, her and Kian helping the younger siblings down the stairs. Once everyone is inside, they spread out and check that they've got the correct bags. To be honest, it's a bit late to go back if they didn't have the correct bag, but we might as well check anyway. Once I get a thumbs up from everyone, I turn to Drew and Ivy.

"Should I deadbolt it?" I ask them.

Ivy nods. "We can't risk The Three figuring out how to get in."

"Nullify it too. We need to be as safe as possible and stay underground for a couple of weeks until everything above ground sorts itself out," Drew says as he goes over to the print scanner.

I nod. "Do it, Drew. Deadbolt and nullify it," I tell him before walking off to check on everyone else.

They all seem settled and content as I watch them explore the safe haven.

"All done," Drew says as he comes to stand next to me. Ivy joins as well, taking up her place on my right.

We don't say anything else as we watch our siblings get used to their new surroundings, and as we begin to realise the amount of responsibility that now sits on our shoulders.

ABOUT THE AUTHOR

A. Carys is a self-published author from Portsmouth, United Kingdom. Other than spending 90% of her day writing, she also loves to crochet, read, and take photos of her family's cats.

Printed in Great Britain
by Amazon